Put Beginning Readers on the Right Track with
ALL ABOARD READING™

The All Aboard Reading series is especially for beginning readers. Written by noted authors and illustrated in full color, these are books that children really and truly *want* to read—books to excite their imagination, tickle their funny bone, expand their interests, and support their feelings. With four different reading levels, All Aboard Reading lets you choose which books are most appropriate for your children and their growing abilities.

Picture Readers—for Ages 3 to 6
Picture Readers have super-simple texts with many nouns appearing as rebus pictures. At the end of each book are 24 flash cards—on one side is the rebus picture; on the other side is the written-out word.

Level 1—for Preschool through First Grade Children
Level 1 books have very few lines per page, very large type, easy words, lots of repetition, and pictures with visual "cues" to help children figure out the words on the page.

Level 2—for First Grade to Third Grade Children
Level 2 books are printed in slightly smaller type than Level 1 books. The stories are more complex, but there is still lots of repetition in the text and many pictures. The sentences are quite simple and are broken up into short lines to make reading easier.

Level 3—for Second Grade through Third Grade Children
Level 3 books have considerably longer texts, use harder words and more complicated sentences.

All Aboard for happy reading!

For
Jane O'Connor
and
Paige Gillies
with thanks.

Thanks! Thanks! Thanks!

Library of Congress Cataloging-in-Publication Data
Holub, Joan.
    Pen pals / by Joan Holub, [author and illustrator.]
        p.   cm. — (All aboard reading. Level 2) "Grades 1-3."
    Summary: Her excitement at having a pen pal quickly turns to disappointment when Daisy, a second-grader, receives some unwelcome news about this new "friend."
    [1. Pen pals—Fiction.   2. Letters—Fiction.   3. Schools—Fiction.]   I. Title.   II. Series.
PZ7.H7427Pe   1997
[E]—dc21   97-5680
                                                                        CIP
ISBN 0-448-41613-1 (GB)   A B C D E F G H I J   AC

ISBN 0-448-41612-3 (pbk)   A B C D E F G H I J

ALL
ABOARD
READING™

Level 2
Grades 1-3

Pen Pals

By Joan Holub

Grosset & Dunlap • New York

"The names of your new pen pals
are in this box,"
Mr. Perry told the class.
Daisy was excited.
She was going to write letters
to her pen pal.
And her pen pal was going
to write back.

Daisy chose a name from the box.

"Becky Benson," she read.

"Who did you get?"

asked Booger Wilcox.

His real name was Wally.

But only Mr. Perry called him that.

Daisy told Booger

the name of her new pen pal.

"Who did you get?" asked Daisy.

"I am not telling," Booger said.

That was just like Booger!

He drove Daisy nuts.

Lisa ran over to them.

"Guess what!" she said.

"My pen pal is named Lisa too!"

Booger waggled his fingers.

"Oooooh," he said in a ghost voice.

"I bet she is your evil twin."

Lisa rolled her eyes.

"Yeah, right," she said.

Mr. Perry clapped his hands.

"Okay, class," he said.

"Quiet down.

Now get ready, get set, WRITE!"

Daisy wrote a letter.

Dear Becky,

My name is Daisy James.
I go to Pine Tree School.
I am in second grade.
My teacher is Mr. Perry.
I like to draw. Do you?

From,
Daisy

She drew daisies on the letter.

It looked cool.

A week later,

letters came from the pen pals.

Daisy read hers.

This is what it said.

Dear Daisy,

My name is not Becky.
It is Bucky.
I am a boy.
I am in second grade
at Willow Tree School.
My teacher is Ms. Flakes.
I like to draw too.

From,
Bucky

P.S. I do not want a girl
for my pen pal.

"My pen pal can do three

cartwheels in a row!" shouted Kyla.

"My pen pal has a treehouse," yelled Ned.

"My pen pal Kirby is

the best hockey player

in his school!" shouted Booger.

It was no fair!

Everyone had a good pen pal but Daisy.

Daisy went to Mr. Perry's desk.

"Can I trade pen pals?" she asked.

Mr. Perry shook his head.

"That might hurt your

pen pal's feelings," he said.

"Try a little harder to make friends."

"Okay," said Daisy.

What else could she do?

Daisy stomped over to the book nook.

Lisa was there.

"My pen pal has red hair," she told Daisy.

"And glasses—just like me."

Booger stopped feeding the hamster.

"Ah-hah!" he butted in.

"I told you she was your evil twin."

"She is not," said Lisa.

But she did not sound so sure.

Lisa looked a little worried.

But Daisy had pen pal

problems of her own.

She went back to her desk.

She wrote another letter.

Dear Bucky,

I do not want a boy
for my pen pal.
But Mr. Perry says
I have to keep you.
We have to write about pets.
My pet is a rat.
His name is Scout.
He runs around my neck.

From,
Daisy

She did not draw

daisies on this letter.

Just for fun,

Daisy got out more paper.

She drew a picture of her rat, Scout.

But she did not send it to Bucky.

It was too good for him.

Daisy took her letter

to the mailbox.

Pen Pal
Mailbox

When she got back,

her rat picture was gone!

It was not on the floor.

Where was it?

After recess,

Daisy saw Booger.

He was snooping at her desk.

Oh, no!

He was reading the letter from Bucky!

Booger smiled.

"You said your pen pal

was a girl," he said.

"But Bucky is a boy."

"Snoop!"

shouted Daisy.

Daisy clobbered him on the back.

Mr. Perry was not around.

That was lucky.

Mr. Perry did not like snooping.

But he did not like clobbering either.

The next week,

more pen pal letters came.

Lisa read hers.

"Oh, no!" she wailed.

"My pen pal has a cat."

"Lots of people have cats," said Daisy.

"A <u>calico</u> cat.

Like I have," said Lisa.

Booger hooted.

"The evil twin strikes again!" he said.

Daisy made a mean face at Booger.

She put her arm around Lisa.

Daisy read Bucky's letter at lunchtime.

Dear Daisy,

I am sending back your
stinky rat picture.
I do not look like a rat.
Here is what I think you
look like—my dog, Beanie.
We have to write
about the summer.
I went to the beach.
I got a ton of shells.

From,
Bucky

P.S. Here is what rhymes
with Daisy—Crazy.

Bucky

How did Bucky get her rat picture?

Daisy had not put Bucky's name on it.

Someone else had done that.

And that same someone

had put it in the mailbox.

Daisy bet she knew who it was.

After lunch, Daisy wrote back to Bucky.

Dear Bucky,

Here is what I did last summer.
I went to see some caves.
People lived in them a long time ago.
Some of their arrows and stuff
are still there.
Somebody else wrote your name
on my rat picture.
Not me.

From,
Daisy

P.S. Here is what rhymes
with Bucky—Yucky!

P.P.S. I do not look like a dog.

Daisy put her letter in the mailbox.

She wished that it was summer right now.

Then she would not have to write

to her dumb pen pal.

On Thursday mornings,

the whole class went to the art room.

Daisy loved art class best of all.

Today the art teacher told the class,

"Draw your favorite animal."

Daisy opened her markers.

"Are you going to draw another rat?"

asked Booger.

"I knew it!" said Daisy.

"<u>You</u> took my rat picture

and mailed it to Bucky.

You are the biggest rat of all!"

Booger did not look sorry.

"Daisy has a boyfriend,"

he started singing.

Daisy pretended that Booger was not there.

Booger began making kissy noises.

But Daisy kept pretending that

she could not hear him.

Booger could not stand it!

The very next day, Mr. Perry

passed out new pen pal letters.

The pen pals had sent school pictures.

Bucky was right.

He did not look like a rat.

Daisy read his letter.

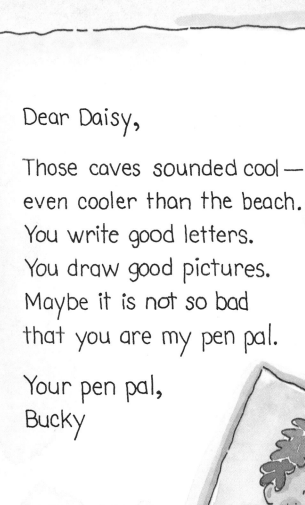

Dear Daisy,

Those caves sounded cool —
even cooler than the beach.
You write good letters.
You draw good pictures.
Maybe it is not so bad
that you are my pen pal.

Your pen pal,
Bucky

"Look at my pen pal's picture," said Lisa.

Lisa's pen pal had red hair and glasses.

But she did not look like Lisa.

"She looks nice," said Daisy.

"Not like an evil twin at all."

Lisa nodded.

They both stared at Booger.

But Booger was looking
at his pen pal's picture.
He was shaking his head.
"Let me see," said Daisy.
"No!" said Booger.

Too late!

Daisy had already seen.

"Ha-ha! Booger's pen pal is a <u>girl</u>!"

shouted Daisy.

"Kirby is a girl!"

Daisy and Lisa smiled big smiles.

"Want to trade?" Booger asked Daisy.

"Then you would have a girl.

And I could have a boy."

Daisy shook her head.

"No way!

I would not stick Bucky with you."

On Saturday, Daisy wrote back to Bucky.

Dear Bucky,

Wally Wilcox is Kirby's pen pal.
He did not know Kirby was a girl.
I did not know you were a boy.
Funny, huh?
Wally wanted to trade pen pals.
But I said no.
I am glad you are my pen pal.

Your pen pal,
Daisy

Uh-oh. She almost forgot.

At the bottom of her letter,

Daisy added one last thing—